The HighBreed and Vilgax are no longer a threat, and the Omnitrix has been destroyed.

Ben Tennyson is now 16 years old, and he must learn the secrets of the new Ultimatrix to battle alien attacks led by the evil Aggregor.

Ben can tap into all of his original powers with the Ultimatrix, but he can also upgrade his alien forms into even STRONGER and more POWERFUL versions – 'ultimate' aliens.

Join the action as Ben goes hero again – ultimate style!

NOW READ ON ...

MEET THE CHARACTERS

Ben Tennyson
He's here to put things right

Gwen Tennyson
Ben's cousin, ready to lend a hand

Kevin E. Levin
He's the muscles of the group

Four Arms
He's a really handy guy

Brain Storm
Ben's cleverest alien

Big Chill
He's an ice cold ghost

Ultimate Big Chill
He can burn and freeze enemies

Humungousaur
He's big, tough and he roars

Ultimate Humungousaur
Bigger than ever, with spikes

iii

Jet Ray
A super-fast swimmer and flyer

Water Hazard
He can fire powerful water blasts

Ultimate Cannonbolt
He likes to roll with it

Magister Gahil
He's a member of the Plumbers

Aggregor
Ben's biggest enemy

iv

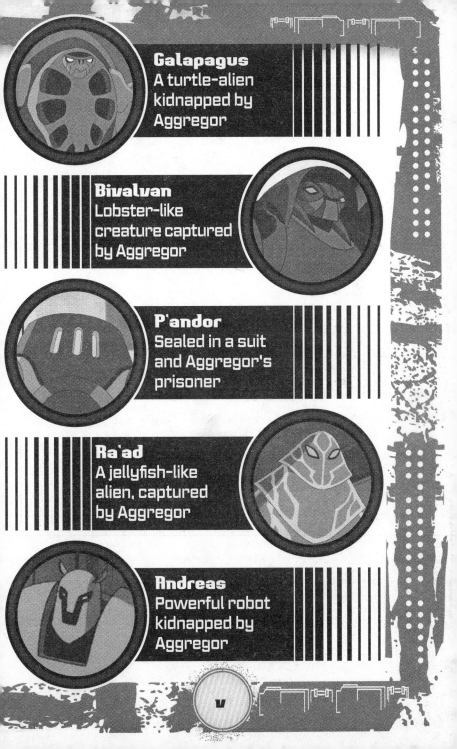

Galapagus
A turtle-alien kidnapped by Aggregor

Bivalvan
Lobster-like creature captured by Aggregor

P'andor
Sealed in a suit and Aggregor's prisoner

Ra'ad
A jellyfish-like alien, captured by Aggregor

Andreas
Powerful robot kidnapped by Aggregor

EGMONT
We bring stories to life

First published in Great Britain 2011
by Egmont UK Limited
239 Kensington High Street
London W8 6SA

Adapted by Barry Hutchison

ISBN 978 1 4052 5977 4

48608/3

Printed and bound in Great Britain

FSC
MIX
Paper
FSC™ C018306

The Forest Stewardship Council (FSC) is an international,
non-governmental organisation dedicated to promoting responsible
management of the world's forests. FSC operates a system of forest
certification and product labelling that allows consumers to identify
wood and wood-based products from well-managed forests.

For more information about Egmont's paper buying policy,
please visit www.egmont.co.uk/ethicalpublishing
For more information about the FSC, please visit
their website at www.fsc.org

CHAPTER ONE

WRONG PLACE AT THE WRONG TIME

Four Arms staggered backwards as a huge, hairy creature punched him hard across the face. Slipping on the snow-covered ground, Four Arms tried hard not to fall. The battle was taking place high up on a mountainside. If he fell, it meant certain death.

'That all you got?' he taunted, when he had regained his balance. The creature he was fighting lashed out with another punch. This one hit him on top of the head, pushing him deep down into the snow.

'Oh, hardly, my dear Ben Tennyson,' said a familiar voice. Dr Animo stepped out from behind the beast. He smiled a wicked smile as he tapped a high-tech headset he wore on his head. 'I've "got" the Yeti's mind.'

Four Arms looked up at the Yeti he was fighting. It was almost twice as big as he was, and three times as strong. A headset, like the one Dr Animo wore, was strapped across its head. A red light shone in the centre of it.

Roaring, Four Arms jumped up. He swung all four fists at the Yeti, ready to deliver a knock-out blow.

Laughing, Dr Animo swung his arms down. The Yeti performed the same move, knocking Four Arms back.

'I, Dr Animo, control the Yeti's every move,' the villain grinned. He kicked his foot out and the Yeti copied. The creature's size twenty-six foot slammed into Four Arms' chest, winding him.

'And I, Dr Animo, will –'

'Dude!' groaned someone nearby. 'Stop saying your name. We know who you are.'

The villain turned to find Kevin glaring at him. Along with Gwen, Kevin was trying to dismantle a house-sized bomb that belonged to Dr Animo. They moved quickly, but carefully. The last thing they wanted to do was set it off.

'I have activated my Devolution Bomb, which shall turn anyone within range of its blasts into a Yeti!' Dr Animo cried, before breaking into a fit of evil laughter.

Four Arms blinked. Gwen and Kevin frowned. Even the Yeti looked unimpressed.

'Seriously?' Four Arms said. 'That's your plan?'

'Kind of reminds you of the old days, doesn't it?' Gwen sighed.

'What, stupid plans?' asked Kevin. 'I guess so.'

Dr Animo's face was red with anger. 'Silence! You won't be so smug once you and everyone else in this hemisphere are all Yetis!'

Controlling the creature's mind, Dr Animo made the Yeti catch hold of Four Arms. The alien hero began to panic when he saw the Yeti's wide mouth and razor-sharp teeth closing in on his head.

CRUNCH!

There was a sudden flash of green light. Just in time, Four Arms transformed into the armour-plated and highly intelligent Brain Storm. The Yeti's teeth cracked on Brain Storm's hard shell.

Howling in pain, the Yeti dropped the alien. Brain Storm's crab-like legs slipped on the snow.

'Hmm, this treacherous terrain indeed poses a dilemma,' he said.

'Shellfish on ice? Delicious,' said Dr Animo. 'Get him!'

The Yeti raced forwards, his big fists raised. Brain Storm waited until he was just a few metres away. 'A battle of brain-power, is it?' he said. 'I'm afraid you, sir, find yourself greatly out-matched.'

His crab shell opened, revealing the enormous brain within. Just as the Yeti was about to attack, a crackle of energy spat from inside Brain Storm's head. It hit the Yeti's headset, turning the light from red to green.

The Yeti stopped running. He

stood still for a moment, swaying gently from side to side. A grin spread across Brain Storm's face.

Spinning around, the Yeti charged at Dr Animo. The villain yelped in fright and stumbled away as quickly as he could. 'No!' he wailed. 'I am your master! Obey me! Heel. Sit. Stay!'

Catching him easily, the Yeti lifted Dr Animo off the ground by one leg. The creature plucked the headset from Dr Animo's head and crushed it between two fingers.

'I'm still paying for that!' Dr Animo sobbed, before he landed, head-first, in the snow.

'Your assistance was greatly appreciated,' Brain Storm told the Yeti. With another blast, he knocked the headset off the creature's head.

'Go now. You are free.'

With one last growl at the evil Dr Animo, the Yeti marched off and vanished into the swirling snow.

'Ah, but you've forgotten one thing,' Animo cried. 'My bomb is still going to go off, and there's nothing you can ...'

His voice trailed off when he spotted the remains of his bomb. The wires had all been pulled out, and the metal shell was lying in pieces on the ground.

'Yeah, taken care of,' Kevin said, putting away his tools.

With a groan, Dr Animo slumped down into the snow.

'Attention, all Plumbers,' said Gwen, speaking into her communicator badge. 'We have a pick up in Sector 7G.'

'Roger that. We're on our way,' said a voice over the communicator.

WHOOSH! A Plumber's spaceship appeared in the sky directly above their heads. 'But why are you guys even out here?' said the voice. 'All the real alien action is going on back in your hometown. In downtown Bellwood!'

Brain Storm, Kevin and Gwen gave one another worried looks. Aliens in Bellwood? That did not sound good!

A news reporter stood in front of a TV camera, talking into a microphone.

'We're live at the scene of destruction here in downtown Bellwood,' he said, 'where what appears to be an alien creature has been going on a rampage!'

SMASH!

An alien who looked like a giant turtle hurled a car through a shop window, making them both explode in a shower of glass. The reporter ducked as the flames shot past him.

CREEERK!

A metal street lamp was bent, then snapped in half by the turtle-alien. He held it like a club, using it to smash the ground in front of him.

At the other end of the street, police cars screeched to a stop. Armed officers jumped out and took cover behind the cars. Raising a large rocket-launcher to his shoulder, one of the policemen took aim, then fired.

The rocket screamed along the street, heading straight towards the rampaging alien. He turned at the last moment, and the rocket exploded against his shell. When the smoke cleared, the alien was still standing.

The news reporter looked into the camera again. 'The one question on everyone's mind,' he said, 'is where is Ben Tennyson?'

CHAPTER TWO

BEN TENNYSON'S RIGHT HERE

The turtle-alien pulled his head back inside his shell, leaving only his arms and legs showing. Leaping into the air, he began to turn. Faster and faster he spun, like a high-powered fan. A strong wind whipped up. It blew along the street, knocking the police back and making them drop their guns.

A bolt of pink energy struck the spinning alien, knocking him to the ground. His head popped up from inside the shell and he saw Gwen, Kevin and Ben standing before him. Brushing his hand against a car, Kevin turned his skin to living metal.

'So, you like a cool breeze, huh?' asked Ben. He turned the dial of the Ultimatrix and a cloud of green energy surrounded him.

'Big Chill!' he cried, unfolding his wings and taking to the air.

The turtle-alien began to garble and growl in a language Ben had never heard before.

'That's what they all say,' Big Chill said. Opening his mouth, he breathed an icy blast of air towards the turtle-alien. It began to spin again, blowing the cold air away.

'OK, so maybe you can hold your own against regular Big Chill,' the hero said. 'But I bet you're no match for ...' He pressed the

Omnitrix symbol on his chest and his blue skin became a bright, fiery red. '… Ultimate Big Chill!'

Raising his fists, Ultimate Big Chill sent fireballs rocketing towards the turtle-alien. As they hit the ground they became sharp ice blades, but the turtle-alien had already rolled to safety.

It stood up quickly and began talking in the same alien language as before.

'You said that already,' said Ultimate Big Chill.

Before the turtle-alien could say anything else, a ball of pink energy surrounded him. He was lifted towards the sky, then he slammed back down onto the concrete.

Stunned, the alien lay on his back, trying to get his breath back.

'Don't you think it's weird how this creature hasn't actually harmed anyone?' Gwen said.

Kevin shook his head. 'Not weird. Just lucky.'

'Really?' Gwen asked. 'Even though it easily could have? It just demolished buildings and cars. No one's that lucky.'

'What, you think it's another baby alien?' asked Ultimate Big Chill, swooping down.

Kevin shuddered. 'I am never

changing a giant nappy again!'

The alien began to get to his feet. Kevin charged, swinging with his metal fists. They bounced harmlessly off the creature's shell. It turned to face him, speaking in its strange alien language again.

'Them's fighting words,' Kevin said. 'Um ... probably.'

'I don't think it's talking to you,' Gwen said. She had noticed that the turtle-alien was staring at Ultimate Big Chill. 'Hey, remember that dragon we fought who turned out to be an alien with a damaged translator?'

'Yeah,' said Ultimate Big Chill, nodding. 'Good times. Good times.'

'Our Plumber's badges work as universal translators. Maybe we should try them now.'

Kevin sighed and took out his badge. 'I swear, if it's another baby ...' he muttered. Activating the badge's translation mode, he pointed it towards the turtle-alien.

'I had no idea how to find you, oh great Ben Tennyson,' the turtle-alien said, as the translator began to work. 'So I thought if I went on a "rampage", the famous hero of Earth would eventually show up to stop me. And here you are!'

Gwen smirked at Kevin. 'Happy?'

Ultimate Big Chill landed next to the alien. 'I have a phone number, you know.' In a flash of green, he turned back to Ben.

'I don't have much time, Ben Tennyson,' the turtle-alien said. 'I urgently need your help!'

The battle was over, but the police, news reporters and a crowd of onlookers stood by, watching to see what would happen next.

'Come on, people,' Kevin said. 'Move along! There's nothing to see here.'

'Except a giant alien monster,' Gwen said, quietly.

'Move along, already,' shouted Kevin. 'Let's go!'

As Kevin shooed the crowds away, Ben questioned the alien. 'Why do you need my help?' he asked. 'You can obviously handle yourself pretty well, Mr ...?'

'Galapagus,' said the alien. 'Violence is not the way of my people.'

Ben glanced around at the ruined street. 'Could've fooled me.'

'I am not here of my own free will,' Galapagus explained. 'But at least I was able to find the great Ben Tennyson, famed in song and story throughout the galaxy.'

'Hear that, guys?' grinned Ben. 'There's a song about me.'

'I am from a peaceful planet called Aldabra,' Galapagus explained. 'Where, like the rest of my people, I ate grass all day and hovered above the ground, enjoying the great gift of life.

'My kind lacks aggression,' he

continued. 'Fighting is not the way of my people. But in my short time on Earth, I've observed that your people fight constantly.'

'Yeah? So how did you know how to fight so well just now?' Kevin demanded.

'I learnt it in prison.'

'I knew this dude couldn't be trusted!' Kevin cried.

Ben raised a hand. 'Er, Kevin?'

'Let me,' said Gwen, swiftly interrupting her cousin. 'Kevin, *you* were in prison.'

Kevin's face fell. 'Oh yeah,' he said. 'Right.'

'One day, a stranger came to our world,' Galapagus went on, 'with the amazing ability to absorb matter and energy, much like your metal friend here.'

'An Osmosian?' Kevin said. 'Doubt it.'

'Lying is not the way of my people,' Galapagus replied. As he continued telling the story, he began to remember every detail, as if he were back there in his home world on the day the mysterious stranger arrived.

He remembered the explosion as the stranger crashed down to the ground, twirling a powerful energy spear. He remembered the screaming and the panic as his family ran for their lives. And he remembered the feeling of terror as the stranger – a horn-headed monster named Aggregor – drained the energy from another Aldabran, leaving behind nothing but a pile of ash on the ground.

CHAPTER THREE

CELL MATES

The awful memories from that day came flooding back to Galapagus. He remembered how Aggregor charged, his energy spear raised. Galapagus spun quickly, flying to safety.

But Aggregor had absorbed the other alien's powers. Six holes appeared in his chest. Strong gales of wind blew from within them, allowing him to fly after Galapagus.

They dodged and weaved through a forest, zooming between trees and beneath high branches. A powerful gust caught Galapagus in mid-air. He yelped in shock as he was knocked back down to the ground. Aggregor touched down next to him and slowly advanced.

'Who are you?' Galapagus whimpered. 'What do you want with me?'

The spear in Aggregor's hands began to glow. Energy fizzled across its metal surface. Galapagus screamed as the power blast hit him. The world went dark and he slumped down into the tall grass, unconscious.

When he opened his eyes

again, Galapagus found a red-shelled lobster-like creature called Bivalvan staring down at him.

'Never seen anything like it,' Bivalvan muttered. He prodded Galapagus with his clawed hand.

'Do you think it can talk?' grunted a voice from the shadows.

Terrified, Galapagus jumped to his feet. His chest vents opened as he got ready to defend himself, but his wind powers refused to work.

A metal hand clamped down on the turtle-alien's shoulder. Galapagus quickly looked up to find P'andor, an alien sealed inside a suit of armour, looming over him. 'Told you, Bivalvan,' P'andor said. 'It's affecting him, too.'

The voice from the shadows spoke again. 'Our abilities don't work in here, either,' it said. A blue jellyfish-like alien named Ra'ad floated from the gloom.

'Andreas is strong,' growled the last occupant of the cell. He was much larger than the rest of them, and looked like some kind of battle robot. He clanged his metal fists together. 'He can bust through these walls!'

Bivalvan pointed to the cell door. A high-tech gizmo was attached to it. It buzzed quietly, sending out some kind of signal.

'No, you can't,' he said. 'Not as long as that thing's stopping our powers working. Think!'

Andreas shook his head. 'I don't like to think.'

Galapagus looked around at the cramped room. 'Bust out of

where?' he asked. 'What exactly is this place?'

'What do you think it looks like, Amphibian Face?' Bivalvan snapped. 'Call it what you want. Jail. Prison. The Big House.'

Galapagus stared back at Bivalvan, blankly.

'Gimme a break, Turtle Boy,' said the armoured P'andor. 'You've never heard of prison?'

'Sorry,' said Galapagus, shaking his head. 'Where I come from, we don't have such a thing.

To restrict another being's freedom? That is unthinkable!'

He looked around at the others. 'My name's not "Turtle Boy" or "Amphibian Face",' he told them. 'It's Galapagus.'

'Andreas thinks Turtle Face is a spy for Aggregor,' Andreas growled, menacingly.

'Aggregor?' asked Galapagus.

'Don't play dumb with us!' said P'andor.

Bivalvan narrowed his eyes. 'You better not be lying.'

Galapagus said the word slowly. 'Ly-ing?'

Ra'ad, the jellyfish creature, snorted loudly. 'Don't tell me you don't have lying where you come from either.'

'No,' admitted Galapagus.

'We have very pleasant weather, though.'

'Why are we wasting our time with this loser?' P'andor asked. 'He can't tell us anything about Aggregor.'

'Aggregor is the alien who captured each of us from our home planets,' Bivalvan explained.

'To siphon our powers for himself, we presume,' Ra'ad continued.

Galapagus remembered what had happened on Aldabra. 'The same creature absorbed my friend's abilities back home,' he said. 'But he seemed only able to use them at a much lesser strength.'

P'andor stroked his armoured chin. 'Interesting.'

'Why would Aggregor kidnap

us at all?' Galapagus wondered. 'Why didn't he just drain us on the spot there and then?'

Bivalvan shrugged. 'Don't know. Not waiting around to find out.' He held up a tiny device. It looked as if it had been built from scraps of metal and other junk.

As the others watched, he attached the device to the transmitter on the cell door.

'You sure we can trust the new guy?' Ra'ad whispered.

P'andor leaned in close to the

jellyfish alien. 'Only as much as we can trust you,' he hissed.

CLICK.

Bivalvan flicked a switch on his home-made gadget and the cell door swished open. Ra'ad turned to leave, but P'andor blocked the way.

'Out of my way, P'andor,' Ra'ad warned. 'I'm the leader here.'

'You're not my leader,' P'andor replied.

CLICK.

Bivalvan flicked the switch in the opposite direction. The gizmo on the cell door stopped buzzing.

'Wait for it ...' Bivalvan muttered. A wave of energy spread from his device, filling the cell.

P'andor held up his hand. It glowed red hot. 'Our powers are back!' he cheered.

'You're welcome,' Bivalvan said. He stepped through the door and out into the corridor.

'I'm following that guy,' Galapagus said, and he and the others joined Bivalvan.

They crept along the corridor, keeping low to avoid being spotted. As they reached the end of the passageway, they stopped. There were a hundred or more robotic soldiers marching towards them. Any second now, they'd be spotted.

Stepping to the front of the group, Andreas stomped his metal foot hard against the ground. The shockwave spread out in front of him, knocking the robots over like skittles.

'We must have hit an asteroid,' droned one of the fallen soldiers.

'Evasive action!'

Clattering noisily, the robots got up and raced away in the opposite direction.

'Asteroid?' Andreas muttered.

'It means "big rock",' said Bivalvan.

'That's bad, right?'

Bivalvan pressed a clawed hand against a wall panel. It blinked and became invisible, revealing the vastness of outer space just beyond.

'This isn't just a prison,' Bivalvan said, realising how terrible their situation was. 'It's a spaceship!'

CHAPTER FOUR

PRISON BREAK

The five escaped prisoners stood at the window, staring out at the distant stars and planets.

'New plan,' said Bivalvan. 'We can't just make a run for it. There's nowhere to run out there, just the void of space.'

'I say we should try to take control of the ship,' P'andor said. 'Who's with me?'

Andreas nodded. 'OK.'

'Think about it, Andreas,' Bivalvan said. 'Nobody knows we've escaped yet. We should keep our advantage as long as we can.'

'Maybe we can send out

a distress signal,' Galapagus suggested.

P'andor looked at them in disgust. 'We've got our powers back. Let's use them to take over!'

'You mean *we've* got our powers back,' Ra'ad said.

Bivalvan nodded. 'You're still trapped inside that suit, and can't really use yours.'

P'andor caught Bivalvan by the arm. Bivalvan hissed in pain as P'andor's hand glowed red hot.

Releasing his grip, P'andor

pushed Bivalvan aside. 'Now,' he snarled, striding off in search of the command deck, 'who's with me?'

Andreas stomped off after P'andor. Shaking his head, Bivalvan went in the opposite direction, with Ra'ad following close behind. Galapagus watched them all leave. He knew he had to choose a side if he was going to survive. But which should he choose?

Up on the command deck, Aggregor sat in his captain's chair, watching stars fly by on a large viewing screen. His robots worked the controls of the ship, steering it safely past asteroids and comets.

Behind him, the door swished open. Andreas entered, swinging his metal fists. He smashed them against the floor, sending another shockwave across the room. Most of the robots fell over, but one managed to stay on its feet. It charged at Andreas, but P'andor stepped up to block its way.

P'andor pressed his hand against the robot's head. His armour became red hot and, with a sizzle, the robot melted into a puddle on the floor.

Aggregor's chair creaked as he slowly turned to face the intruders. His mouth curved into a nasty smile. 'A prison break, is it?' he snarled.

Down at his side, his energy spear sparked into life.

On another deck, more robots were in the communications room. They wore headsets, listening for any signals from the dark depths of space.

They didn't notice a puddle of water seep under the door. It crept across the floor, silently flooding the room around them.

BZZZZZZT!

An electrical charge raced across the water. It hit the robots, short-circuiting their wiring. With a splash, they all hit the floor at the same time.

The door suddenly opened, revealing Bivalvan and Ra'ad. A whirring shape passed above them as Galapagus flew into the room. He landed beside one of the control panels and leaned in to a microphone.

'Mayday, mayday,' he said. 'Any Plumbers in the vicinity, please respond.'

He listened for a reply, but heard only the hiss of radio static.

'Did I say it right, Bivalvan?' he asked. 'That's the word you wanted me to use? Plumbers?'

Two loud zaps from behind him made Galapagus jump. He turned in time to see Bivalvan and Ra'ad slump down onto the floor. Aggregor stood over them, his energy spear still sizzling.

'If you and your little friends are through with this pathetic exercise, you may rejoin your fellow inmates back in your cell,' Aggregor growled. 'Guards!' he shouted, and a squad of robotic soldiers rushed into the room.

A thousand miles away, a distress signal lit up on the control console of a Plumber's spaceship. At the flick of a switch, an image of Aggregor's ship appeared on the view screen.

'Hailing unidentified space starcruiser in sector 18404. This is Magister Prior Gahlil of the Plumbers. We have received your distress call. Prepare to be boarded.'

The Plumber's ship closed the gap in the blink of an eye. Cutting the power, Magister Gahlil touched down on the landing strip of Aggregor's much bigger spaceship.

Climbing down from inside his own vehicle, Gahlil came face to face with Aggregor and some more of his robotic soldiers. 'The distress call was a computer error,' Aggregor explained. 'Everything's fine here.'

Gahlil looked at Aggregor suspiciously. 'Then you won't mind if I have a look around.'

Aggregor hesitated, then nodded. 'Of course not, Magister.'

Back in the cell, the five prisoners were crammed together

once again. Bivalvan's gadget had been removed from the door, allowing the jamming device to block their powers.

'Brilliant plan, P'andor,' Bivalvan grunted.

'Like you did any better?'

'If you hadn't alerted Aggregor to our escape, someone would have come to help us by now!'

P'andor clenched his fists. 'We could have taken him out on the bridge if you'd all been there to fight, too!'

The cell door slid open. Magister Gahlil stared in at the prisoners. 'And what do we have here?' he asked.

The five captives cheered with relief when they spotted the Plumber uniform. 'We're saved!' cried Galapagus.

Bivalvan gave P'andor a nudge. 'See, I told you my plan was better.'

Gahlil looked around at the cramped cell. 'This is a clear violation of Code T22 dash – **RRGH!**'

A bolt of electrical energy hit Gahlil on the back. The Plumber toppled forwards, unconscious. The prisoners looked up to see Aggregor grinning back at them.

'Who's next?' he asked.

All five captives stepped free

of the cell. Out of the jamming device's range, their powers began to return. Bivalvan attacked first, raising his hands and spraying a high-powered jet of water at Aggregor.

Before the water hit him, two robot soldiers slid in front of it, protecting their master.

ZZZRP!

Energy shot from the end of Aggregor's spear. Andreas smashed his fists against the wall, bringing large chunks of the ceiling falling down. They landed in front of Bivalvan, saving him from Aggregor's blast.

'Careful, Andreas,' Bivalvan warned. 'We're on a spaceship. You'll breach the hull!' He pointed to the floor, where a small crack was growing steadily wider.

'He's not going to destroy us,' P'andor spat. 'If he wanted us dead, he'd have done it a long time ago.'

'You're smarter than you look,' Aggregor nodded.

Galapagus swallowed, nervously. 'After you absorb our powers, you're going to let us go, right?'

Aggregor laughed. He raised his spear above his head. 'After I drain your powers, there won't be anything left of you!' he said, and with that, he prepared to fire.

CHAPTER FIVE

THE DOUBLE CROSS

The crack in the floor split into a wide hole, just as Aggregor got ready to attack. Moving quickly, Ra'ad, P'andor, Andreas and Bivalvan leapt through the gap, landing on the deck below.

Only Galapagus remained, too frightened to fight or flee. He curled up inside his shell, hoping Aggregor wouldn't hurt him too badly.

On the lower deck, the others had realised that Galapagus was missing. 'Where's Turtle Face?' Andreas asked.

'Aggregor has him,' Bivalvan said. He darted along the corridor. 'Move!'

The others raced after him. At the end of the corridor, Ra'ad spotted some electrical cables. Using his own electric powers, he zapped the cables. The lights on the ship suddenly went dim, giving them shadow to hide in.

'This way to the bridge,' P'andor said, as he spotted another corridor he recognised. They all followed, sticking close to the walls and using the shadows for cover.

Aggregor's voice hissed at them over hidden speakers. 'Rats in a maze,' he laughed.

Realising they were being watched, Andreas smashed through a wall, creating a shortcut. 'Seriously, Andreas,' muttered Ra'ad, floating through the hole, 'stop smashing the ship. I like breathing.'

A large shape came racing towards them through the darkness. They raised their fists, ready to fight, then lowered them again when they saw Galapagus.

'He's right behind me!' cried Galapagus, glancing back over his shoulder.

'In here!' barked P'andor, pulling the others through a door he knew led onto the command deck.

They huddled together inside the door, watching for any sign of Aggregor. When they eventually heard his voice, it was from right behind them.

'When Osmosians absorb the energy of other life forms, we only gain one-tenth of that creature's abilities.'

The prisoners turned to find Aggregor standing in the middle of the command deck. 'But I have a better way. I've built a machine back on my home planet that will allow me to absorb *all* of your powers.'

Bivalvan raised his hands to fire a water blast, but only a trickle emerged. Ra'ad's electrical abilities were fading, too. Andreas and

P'andor could also feel their own powers drain away.

'Now that this little diversion has ended, that is precisely where we're headed,' Aggregor said.

Bivalvan, Ra'ad, P'andor and Andreas turned to find Galapagus holding up the jamming device.

'Turtle Face stole our powers?' said Andreas.

'Turtle Face blocked your powers,' Aggregor corrected. '*I* am going to steal them.'

Robotic soldiers rushed in and threw the prisoners to the ground. 'Traitor!' roared P'andor, as he was hurled to the floor.

'Once I have all your powers combined, nothing can stop me from attaining the ultimate prize!' Aggregor said.

Galapagus slowly raised a hand. 'Except me. You promised to release me if I helped you capture the others.'

Aggregor sneered. 'I lied.'

'What a coincidence,' said Galapagus. 'I lied, too.'

A gust of air blasted from within his chest cavity. It carried the jamming device across the command deck. Aggregor gave a grunt as the device hit him so hard on the chest that it stuck to his rough skin.

With the device draining away every one of his stolen powers, Aggregor fell to his knees. He struggled to pull the jamming device off, but it was stuck tight.

Leaping high up into the air, Galapagus unleashed another wind attack. This one was directed at the robot soldiers. It lifted them off their feet, before smashing them to pieces against the walls.

Bivalvan stood up and nodded his approval. 'I'm following *that* guy,' he said, and they all raced as fast as they could towards one of the escape pods.

The escape pod streaked away from Aggregor's ship. It raced towards a distant blue and green planet, where the former prisoners hoped they would be safe.

KA-BLARRM!

A laser cannon on Aggregor's ship blasted away one of the escape pod's wings. The pod shook violently as it entered the planet's atmosphere and plunged towards the ground.

KR-BOOOM!

The pod crashed down on a beach, spraying sand in all directions. All five of the escaped prisoners pulled themselves free of the wreckage, shaken but unhurt.

'Everybody all right?' asked Galapagus.

'Not for long,' Ra'ad replied. 'Aggregor will soon be in pursuit.'

'We've got to split up,' said P'andor, quickly.

Bivalvan shook his head. 'Negative. We stay with the escape pod. It's our only way off this world.'

'Suit yourself,' shrugged P'andor. There was no way he was sticking around.

Galapagus shook the hands of his new friends. 'May we meet again, in this life or a better one,' he said.

Leaving Bivalvan behind, the others headed off across the beach, and all went their separate ways.

Ben, Gwen and Kevin listened to the story, fascinated.

'And I haven't seen any of them since,' Galapagus told them.

'That's the crash site in Florida

where we found Bivalvan,' Ben said excitedly.

'He's still there?'

'No. Plumbers took him off planet Earth,' said Kevin.

'We helped him get home and now it's your turn,' said Gwen. She took out her Plumbers badge and used it to signal for a transport ship.

'I am profoundly grateful to you all,' Galapagus said.

'Just one more thing,' Ben said, pressing a button on the Ultimatrix. A yellow light scanned Galapagus from head to foot.

'Uncatalogued DNA detected,' chimed the Ultimatrix. There was a pause, then: 'Unknown DNA sample acquired. Scan complete.'

Ben smiled. Another alien added to the collection. 'Sweet,' he

said, then he and the others said
their goodbyes.

The Plumber's ship soared
away from Earth. Galapagus stood
by the window, watching the planet
grow steadily smaller.

'I can't thank you Plumbers
enough for taking me home,' he
said, finally.

Up in front, the pilot slowly
removed his helmet. Galapagus
gasped when a horned head was
revealed.

Aggregor turned in the seat
and grinned, wickedly. 'Who says
you're going home?' he cackled, as
he flew them both deeper into the
dark, cold emptiness of space.

Ultimate Big Chill is set for battle

Aggregor attacks Galapagus

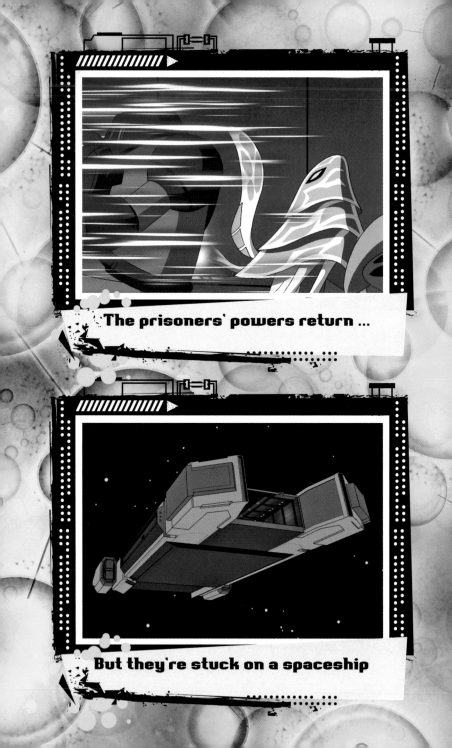

The prisoners' powers return ...

But they're stuck on a spaceship

Aggregor confronts his prisoners

And Galapagus leads an attack

The escape pod hurtles to Earth

The Ultimatrix has a new alien

P'andor is tough to crack

Ultimate Humungousaur takes aim

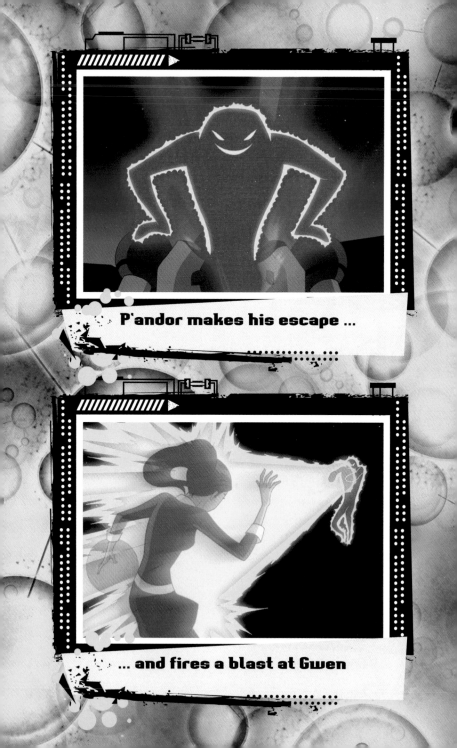

P'andor makes his escape ...

... and fires a blast at Gwen

Water Hazard's on the scene

P'andor feeds on nuclear energy

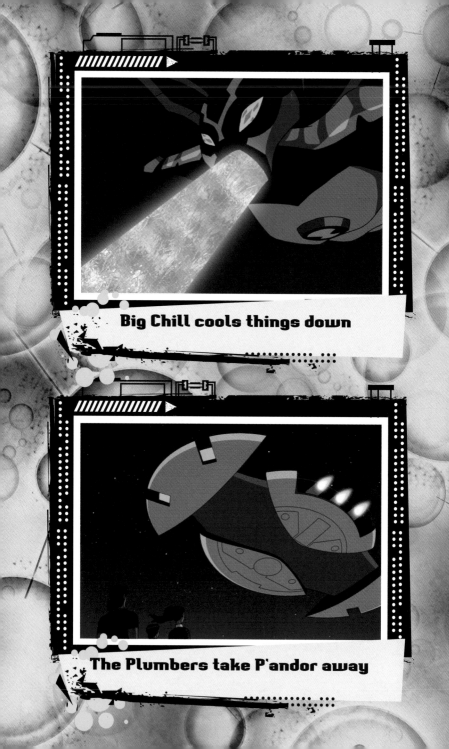

Big Chill cools things down

The Plumbers take P'andor away

BEN 10
ULTIMATE
ALIEN

TOO
HOT TO
HANDLE

CHAPTER ONE

IF I HAD A HAMMER

A hulking brute of a man pushed open the doors of an old warehouse and stepped inside. His name was Hammer, after the heavy sledgehammer he always carried with him.

There were two other men in the warehouse already. One was grey-haired and dressed like a surgeon. The other had a spiky Mohican and carried a power saw. He'd painted his name – Buzz – on the handle.

The sound of drilling echoed around the warehouse as Hammer

approached the other men. 'You guys here for the safe-cracking job?' he asked.

The surgeon nodded, and Hammer joined the back of the queue. 'So,' he said, 'what's the story about this guy?'

Buzz looked up a set of stairs, to where the drilling sounds were coming from. 'He's shelling out a cool million to bust open a safe. That's all anybody needs to know.'

BOOOOM!

An explosion rocked the warehouse. Hammer and the others watched as another man flew over their heads. He crashed against the back wall of the warehouse, then fell to the floor.

'Next!' bellowed a voice from the top of the stairs.

The surgeon didn't wait to be told twice. He hurried up the steps, stopping when he reached the top. A metal-clad figure sat on a large, throne-like chair. It was P'andor, sealed inside his suit of armour.

So where's the safe that needs cracking?' the surgeon asked.

'You're looking at it.'

The surgeon paused, then nodded. 'OK,' he said, removing a surgical blade from inside his coat. At the press of a button, the blade began to glow with alien energy.

Moving with great skill, the surgeon sliced at the armour. But no matter how many places he tried to cut through, the metal suit showed no signs of damage. 'What is this made of?' he gasped.

P'andor sighed. 'Next!'

'This should be fun!' cried Buzz, racing up the steps. His power saw roared into life and he set to work trying to cut open P'andor's armour. The saw blade shattered almost straight away, without leaving a scratch on the armour.

'I've got another blade right here,' Buzz said, but P'andor wasn't interested.

'Next!'

CLANG!

The hammer smashed against

the side of P'andor's head. The
armoured alien didn't budge.

CLANG! CLANG! CLANG!

Again and again it struck him,
until Hammer dropped to his knees,
too tired to continue.

'Next!' boomed P'andor. No
one appeared at the top of the
stairs. 'I said *next!*'

There was the sound of
footsteps slowly climbing the stairs.
A young man finally appeared, his
long black hair hanging around
his shoulders. He carried a toolbox
in one hand. His name had been
scratched into the metal: Kevin.

'Sorry,' Kevin said, smirking.
'Am I late?'

Kevin set his toolbox down
on the floor and opened the lid. A
large green diamond lay inside,

between the tools and Kevin's Plumber's badge. As he brushed his hand against the diamond, his skin became as hard as its shiny surface.

P'andor leaned forward in his chair. 'I didn't realise there was an Osmosian on this planet,' he said. 'Or a supply of Taydenite.'

Kevin's right arm stretched out until it looked like a long sword. He turned to Hammer and the others. 'You guys might want to move back a bit.'

KRRISSH!

The blade sliced through the chest plate of P'andor's armour. Kevin grinned. 'That's one million in cash, right?'

Suddenly, Kevin's Plumber badge flashed red and a high-pitched alarm began to squeal. Kevin looked over at it, then back at the cut in the armour.

'**Radiation?**' he said, frowning. 'What you got in there, big guy?'

'**Don't** ask questions,' P'andor growled. 'Just open it!'

Kevin pulled back. 'Don't think so. Not until you tell me what's going on here.'

'**You** open this suit, I pay you. That's all you need to know.'

Kevin picked up his toolbox and started to leave. 'That's not how I do business.' He nodded as

he passed the other safe-crackers.
'Gentlemen.'

'**One** hundred thousand dollars
to whoever stops him!' P'andor
cried, leaping to his feet.

All three thugs immediately
moved to attack. Kevin ducked as
Hammer's hammer arced towards
him, then rolled to avoid a swipe
from the surgeon's energy blade.
The toolbox clattered to the ground,
spilling its contents over the floor.

The surgeon and Hammer
charged again, but Kevin was ready

for them. His foot crunched against the surgeon's jaw, then a fist slammed into Hammer's stomach, doubling him over.

Buzz screamed with laughter as he swung the new blade of his power saw towards Kevin's head. Sparks began to fly as Kevin blocked the attack with his diamond-hard arms.

'Wasting your time, fellas,' Kevin said. 'Nothing's harder than Taydenite.'

WHUMP!

A hammer blow hit Kevin on the side of the head, knocking him over. Stunned, he lost control of his powers. His skin returned to its normal colour as the Taydenite shielding wore off.

The three thugs advanced, their weapons raised. Defenceless, Kevin could only run. Stopping only to grab his Plumber badge, Kevin bounded down the stairs and hurried out through the front door of the warehouse.

Buzz fired up his power saw. 'Do I still get the hundred grand if I bring him back in pieces?'

'Let him go!' bellowed P'andor. He stooped and picked up the Taydenite from the floor where it had been dropped. 'I have everything I need.'

CHAPTER TWO

DRILL OF DESTRUCTION

Ben's car drove up the ramp of the Rustbucket III spaceship and stopped. The doors opened and Ben and Gwen stepped out. They looked worried.

'Any sign of our alien fugitives?' Gwen asked.

'Nothing,' replied Ben. 'Maybe Kevin's had better luck.'

'We should have heard from him by now,' said Gwen. 'It's not like him not to call.'

'What do you mean? It's totally like him not to call.'

'I meant to not call *me*,' said Gwen.

With a sharp screech of tyres, Kevin's car appeared at the top of the ramp. It skidded to a stop right in front of them. 'I found one of our missing aliens,' he said, stepping from inside the car. He held up his Plumber's badge and a hologram of P'andor appeared. 'This one's hot,' he warned. 'Really hot.'

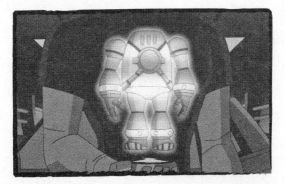

'P'andor?' said Ben, leaning in to get a closer look at the image. 'Whatever he is inside that armour, we do not want to let him out,' Kevin said.

'So how can we help him?' asked Gwen.

'Help him?' Kevin spluttered. 'I'm going back there and putting a beating on him. Are you guys with me or what?'

'We're supposed to be rescuing the escaped aliens,' Gwen reminded him. 'Not attacking them.'

Kevin shrugged. 'Fine, rescue what's left after I pound him.'

'I hate to take sides,' said Ben, 'but Kevin's right.'

'He is?'

'I am?'

'Well, half right. We need to go back there. To investigate.'

'Fine, we'll investigate,' Kevin said. 'Then we'll pound him.'

The three heroes stood in the warehouse, looking around. Gwen used her Plumber's badge to scan for anything suspicious.

'I'm not picking up any radiation,' she said. 'You sure this is the right place?'

Kevin nodded. 'Yeah. And we need to find P'andor fast. Before he escapes from that armour.'

'I thought nothing could penetrate it?' said Ben.

Kevin pointed down to his open toolbox. 'Except the Taydenite sample I accidentally left behind.'

Ben looked puzzled. 'Why were you searching for alien fugitives with a Taydenite sample?'

'I might not have exactly been searching for aliens,' Kevin admitted. 'I mean, I was at first. Then I heard a rumour about a guy offering big money to bust open a … difficult thing to bust open.'

'And so you thought you'd pick up some extra cash by irradiating an entire city?'

'I didn't open it, did I?' said Kevin, defensively.

Ben pulled an angry face. 'No, you just left behind the one thing he needed to do it himself. And now we have no idea how to find him.'

'Yes we do,' said Gwen. Her eyes were glowing with magical pink energy as she pressed her fingertips against the lid of the toolbox. 'Whoever touched this case last? He's close.'

Deep in an underground tunnel, a drilling machine moved slowly forwards. The big drill was spinning, cutting a hole through the tunnel wall. A workman sat inside, whistling as he worked the controls.

'Whoa! Stop! Shut it off!'

The driver looked down to find his boss standing beside the vehicle. He was holding up a Geiger counter, a device used to detect radiation. It was making a loud clicking noise. Warning lights were flashing all over the device.

'Did we just strike uranium?' he asked. 'Radiation levels are spiking like crazy. We need to clear out of here right –'

KABOOM!

The opposite wall exploded, showering the workmen in dust. When it had settled, P'andor, Hammer, Buzz and the surgeon stood in the hole. Buzz raised his saw and ran at the workers, laughing crazily.

'Get away from the drill!' he

screeched. 'I'd hate to mess up my nice new buzz-saw.'

As the workers ran for their lives, P'andor and the others took control of the drill vehicle. The surgeon jumped into the driver's seat while the others held onto the outside.

Crunching the gears, the surgeon steered the drill along a side tunnel. The vehicle's tracks trundled along the rocky path, bouncing the passengers around.

Suddenly, an enormous

shape blocked the drill's path. The surgeon slammed on the brakes, bringing the drill to a stop just a few metres away from the dino-alien, Humungousaur.

'Road's closed, losers,' Humungousaur growled. Kevin and Gwen stood beside him, ready for anything.

'Out of our way!' P'andor commanded. He jumped down from the vehicle, with Hammer and Buzz following closely behind.

With a roar of rage, Hammer smashed his sledgehammer down on Humungousaur's foot. The dino-alien gave a yelp of pain and began hopping around, holding his big toe.

CRUNCH! Humungousaur fell, butt-first, onto Hammer, flattening him against the ground. Hammer groaned loudly, but didn't get up.

Giggling, Buzz swung at Gwen with his saw. She blocked the attack with an energy shield. A second later, Humungousaur's tail smacked into Buzz, sending him crashing into the tunnel wall.

Slamming down on the accelerator, the surgeon drove the drill straight towards the giant Humungousaur. The alien managed to catch hold of the vehicle. His muscles strained as he struggled to hold it back.

Meanwhile, Kevin was closing in on P'andor. Touching the tunnel wall, his body turned to living stone. He changed his hand into a large, spiky mace. 'I want that Taydenite back,' he said, charging.

Just before he reached

P'andor, a wall of pink energy
appeared in front of him. His
face smacked against it and he
staggered back.

'We should try talking before
we start hitting,' Gwen said.

Kevin smashed the energy
field. 'It works better for me the
other way around.'

Gwen ignored him and walked
over to P'andor. 'It's all right,' she
said. 'We know you're on the run
from Aggregor. We've already
helped two of your friends. We're

not here to hurt you. We just want to help you get home.'

P'andor seemed to think about this. 'If you really want to help, then free me from this armour. I am starving inside this prison.'

Closing her eyes, Gwen raised one hand. P'andor's armour glowed with a pink light.

'Don't!' Kevin cried, shoving her aside. Her concentration broken, the pink energy faded away.

'What are you doing?' Gwen demanded.

'I'm telling you, you don't want to bust that thing open.'

'Busting things is your job,' Gwen said. She raised her hand again and the pink light returned. 'I was just trying to read the armour. Figure out how it works.'

BZZZZZT!

An energy feedback crackled from the armour. It hit Gwen hard, catapulting her backwards.

'What did you do to her?' Kevin roared. He slammed punch after punch against P'andor's chest. The armoured alien didn't seem to feel them. With a sharp movement of one arm, P'andor sent Kevin crashing after Gwen.

Humungousaur watched the others hit the ground. He was still struggling to hold back the deadly drill, and now Hammer and Buzz were attacking again, too.

He gave a low growl. He had had enough of this.

It was time to go Ultimate!

CHAPTER THREE

BREAKING FREE

The drill vehicle was hurled backwards as Humungousaur transformed into his Ultimate form. His already huge muscles doubled in size as his skin went from brown to a dark green. Spikes grew from his back and from the end of his powerful tail.

'Ultimate Humungousaur!' he bellowed, in a voice loud enough to shake the walls.

The dino-alien raised one arm. His hand became like putty, changing shape until it formed the outline of a cannon. Missiles rocketed from within. They rained down around P'andor and the other villains, driving them back.

'You mess with my friends, you mess with –' Ultimate Humungousaur stopped, mid-sentence, when he realised he'd made a terrible mistake. The rockets had damaged the tunnel, and now it was collapsing all around them!

Stretching up, he pressed his hands against the ceiling, before it could fall on Kevin and Gwen and crush them. 'Got it!' he said, struggling with the weight. A small rock fell from the ceiling. It bounced off Kevin's head with a thonk.

'Ow!'

'Sorry.'

'I forgive you,' said Kevin. 'Anybody can make a mistake.'

'Like leaving the Taydenite behind?' said Gwen.

Kevin smiled. 'For instance.'

Ultimate Humungousaur groaned. He'd been so busy holding up the roof, he hadn't noticed the villains drilling another hole through the wall.

'P'andor got away with the drill,' he said.

'Only because you guys have been thinking with your fists instead of your brains,' snapped Gwen.

'And what were you thinking with when you tried to help him?' asked Kevin. A glowing platform appeared beneath his and Gwen's feet and slowly lifted them towards the ceiling. Ultimate Humungousaur was still holding it in place.

'I'm thinking he's scared, on the run from Aggregor, and probably starving to death,' Gwen said. 'Wouldn't you be desperate to get out of that armour?'

'So, desperate makes him trustworthy?' Kevin asked.

'He'll never trust us if we keep attacking him.'

'Ever think he's sealed inside that armour for a reason?'

'Guys?' said Ultimate Humungousaur, interrupting their argument. 'I'm getting cramp here.'

Kevin pressed his hands against the ceiling, and used his powers to fuse the cracks in the stone together. The dino-alien's muscles relaxed and the roof stayed in place.

'He's radioactive,' Kevin continued. 'If we let him out of that suit, he'll kill everyone who comes near him.'

'So we let him starve to death?' Gwen demanded. 'That's cold, even for you.'

'Not cold. Sensible. You're the one who's not thinking strai–'

The energy platform tipped sideways, sending Kevin thudding down onto the ground. 'You did that on purpose!' he cried.

'I wasn't concentrating,' Gwen said, but Kevin knew she was lying.

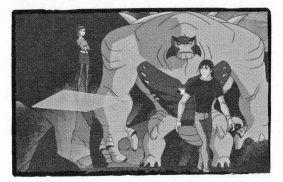

'That's it,' he said. Brushing himself down, he stomped off through the tunnel. 'I'm outta here.'

BRRRRRK!

In a quarry just beyond the tunnels, the drill began to spin against P'andor's chest plate. The Taydenite was attached to the drill's point. It tore at the metal armour, scratching its surface.

'At last!' P'andor cried, but his excitement was cut short when –

KER-ACK!

The strain of trying to cut through the armour shattered the drill to pieces. Buzz and Hammer ducked as shards of metal came whizzing past their heads. The Taydenite landed on the ground, undamaged.

'We're going to need another drill,' the surgeon said.

'No,' said P'andor. 'We need the Osmosian.'

Kevin's car cruised along a deserted road. Behind the steering wheel, Kevin muttered angrily to himself. He was still annoyed at Gwen for knocking him off the platform.

A movement in his rear view

mirror caught his attention. The drill truck raced up behind him, the drill itself hanging in pieces. Before he could speed away, the truck pulled in front of him, blocking his escape.

There was a loud **THUD** as Buzz landed on the roof of the car. Kevin looked up in time to see a spinning saw blade slice through the roof.

'This is just what I need!' he groaned, leaning right to avoid the dangerous blade.

SMASH!

Hammer swung down from the truck, shattering Kevin's window with his sledgehammer. Unable to see, Kevin swerved all over the road. Buzz leapt to safety just as the car hit a verge and flipped over onto its roof.

Hanging upside down inside the car, an unconscious Kevin gave a low groan. The drill truck came to a stop. Hammer and the surgeon stepped down.

Buzz revved up his chainsaw and approached the upturned car. 'Let's open him up and see what's inside,' he sniggered.

'Wait!' the surgeon cried, stopping Buzz in his tracks. He looked down at Kevin. 'We need him alive!'

Kevin's head ached when he opened his eyes. That was the least of his worries. He was lying on the ground of the abandoned quarry, with P'andor standing over him.

'Time to finish the job you started, Osmosian,' said the armoured alien. He dropped the Taydenite at Kevin's feet.

Kevin picked up the green diamond. 'How stupid do you think I am?'

'Stupid enough to get caught,' said the surgeon. Kevin looked over to him. All three thugs were standing together, watching on.

'Stupid enough to pass up a million bucks,' Buzz added.

'Stupid enough to take us on,' finished Hammer.

Buzz raised his power saw. 'Come on, ya lousy freak.'

'What are you ...' snorted Hammer. 'Afraid?'

The surgeon laughed. 'Your little girlfriend would put up more of a fight.'

That was it! Furious, Kevin absorbed the Taydenite's power. His skin turned a shiny green and his arms became two long, thin blades. He raced at the three villains, roaring angrily and swinging with his arms.

SNIK!

P'andor stepped in front of
Kevin just as he swung. The blades
sliced through the front of the
armour as if it were soft butter.

'Also?' said the alien. 'You're
stupid enough to do that!'

As the armour fell apart, a
flaming figure flew out from within.
P'andor's whole body burned super-
hot as he streaked up towards the
sky, free at last!

CHAPTER FOUR

AIR-TO-AIR BATTLE

P'andor darted across the sky above the quarry, whooshing and zooming in all directions.

'Finally!' he cheered. 'I am no longer bound by the shackles of that armour!'

Back down on the ground, Kevin changed into his normal form. The glow of headlights dazzled him as Ben's car pulled up. Gwen hurried over to his side.

'Kevin, are you all right?' she asked.

'I'm OK. But I thought you were mad at me?'

'More like afraid you'd do something stupid,' replied Gwen, softly.

P'andor zoomed by overhead. 'Good call,' Kevin mumbled.

Ben pulled up his sleeve and twisted the Ultimatrix. 'Nothing I can't handle,' he said, but before he could transform, the Ultimatrix began to flash yellow.

'Uncatalogued DNA detected,' it said.

'Not now,' Ben groaned.

Gwen looked up to the sky,

where P'andor was looping and swooping with delight. 'He's just celebrating,' she said. 'He hasn't done anything.'

Creating an energy platform, Gwen floated up into the evening air. As she drew closer to P'andor, her Plumber's badge flashed a radiation warning.

'Your natural form is harmful to humans,' she told him. 'We can arrange a ride home for you.'

The crackling flames of P'andor's face changed to form a

wicked smile. 'Now, why would I ever go home?' he asked. He took hold of an overhead electrical power cable. At once, its energy began to flow into him. 'This planet is like an all-you-can-eat buffet!'

A yellow beam shot from the Ultimatrix. It passed through P'andor, startling him.

'Unknown DNA sample acquired,' chimed the watch. The light on its front turned green again. 'Scan complete.'

'Your weapon can't hurt me,' P'andor growled.

Gwen raised her hands, defensively. 'It's not a wea–'

A blast of radioactive energy struck her, knocking her from the platform. She fell, limply, towards the distant ground.

'Jet Ray!'

Leaping into the air, Jet Ray flew faster than he'd ever flown before. A split-second before Gwen hit the ground, Jet Ray's claws tightened around her shoulders. He banked sharply in the sky, then gently set her down beside Kevin.

Kevin put his arms around Gwen, holding her as she woke up.

Meanwhile, Jet Ray was closing in on P'andor. He spread his wings wide, planning to hit the villain at full speed. But instead of crashing into P'andor, he passed straight through him.

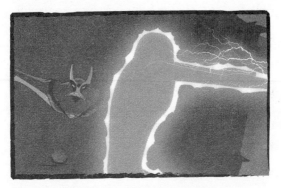

Jet Ray performed a perfect loop, circling around to face P'andor. 'You can't stay on Earth,' he shouted. 'Your radiation will eventually kill us.'

'Let me speed up the process,' P'andor said. He fired a series of energy bolts in Jet Ray's direction. The alien hero dodged and weaved, avoiding the shots.

Then it was Jet Ray's turn. He let loose with a neuro-shock blast.

It hit P'andor, but was immediately absorbed into the alien's burning body.

'I appreciate the snack, Aerophibian,' he cackled, firing another burst of energy. It caught Jet Ray's wings, sending him flipping over and over through the air. 'But I sense a full meal nearby.'

P'andor looked around him. Beyond the quarry, he could make out the twin chimneys of a nuclear power station. His eyes blazed with pure greed as he rocketed towards the closest chimney.

From down on the ground, the surgeon gave a shout. 'Does this mean we're not getting paid?'

One of P'andor's blasts streaked down from the sky. It hit the ground at the surgeon's feet, sending him, Buzz and Hammer sprawling in a cloud of dust.

Hammer sighed. 'I think that will be a "no".'

Not too far away from the fallen thugs, Kevin helped Gwen to her feet. 'Go ahead,' said Gwen. 'Say "I told you so".'

'Forget it,' said Kevin, smiling. 'You're almost always right, and you never call me on it. I do have a plan, though.'

Touching P'andor's armour, he changed his skin into the ultra-tough metal. Concentrating hard, he used his abilities to weld the damaged armour back together until it was almost as good as new.

Right at that moment, P'andor was closing in on the power plant. Jet Ray raced after him. His mind was racing just as fast, trying to figure out what he should do.

'So how do you stop an alien you can't even touch?' he wondered. 'What would Gwen do? Make friends with him? That's stupid.' An idea popped into his head. 'Wait, maybe not. He's already got friends on Earth ...'

P'andor zipped through the air, his eyes locked on the power station. A shout from a familiar voice broke his concentration and made him stop.

'P'andor! It's me,' said Water Hazard, perched on a nearby wall. Unknown to P'andor, Ben had used the Ultimatrix to turn into Water Hazard, Bivalvan's form. 'This planet's a waste of time. Take some advice from a friend and go home.'

'Bivalvan?' P'andor frowned.
'I thought you'd already found a
way home. In any case, this doesn't
concern you.'

'I can't let you stay here,'
Water Hazard warned.

P'andor shrugged and
continued on his way towards the
power plant. 'It's not up to you.'

SKOOOSH!

Twin jets of water shot
from Water Hazard's hands. They
hit P'andor, knocking him to the
ground. The heat of P'andor's body

quickly turned the water to steam. In moments, Water Hazard was barely able to see a thing.

'Maybe not the best strategy,' he muttered, before a shape sprang from within the cloud of steam. P'andor's punch was so powerful, it knocked Water Hazard through one of the power station's walls.

Inside the station, emergency alarms began to sound. The scared workers and scientists inside ran for the exits as P'andor stomped inside.

Stepping over the fallen Water Hazard, P'andor crossed to an electrical turbine. He plunged his hands into the machinery, and laughed as the power flowed into his body.

'Yes!' he cried. 'Sweet, pure energy!'

And with that, P'andor began to grow.

CHAPTER FIVE

RADIOACTIVE MAN

An alarm from the Ultimatrix woke Water Hazard. He looked over at P'andor, then down at the flashing symbol on his chest. 'Radiation level's off the scale,' he said. 'Better cool this guy down.'

With a tap of the Ultimatrix, Water Hazard became Big Chill. Unfurling his wings, he flew straight at P'andor. He left a thin layer of ice behind when he phased through the villain's body.

'You dare interrupt my meal?' P'andor roared. He fired an energy blast at Big Chill, only for it to pass right through him.

'I can't touch you, you can't touch me,' Big Chill explained. Opening his mouth, he blew a gust of icy wind in P'andor's direction. The radioactive menace dodged to the side, then flew back towards the hole in the wall.

Another freezing breath swirled down from above. This one found its target. For a moment, P'andor found himself trapped in a lump of ice. The ice shattered, then melted away as he bounced off the floor.

A look of panic passed across P'andor's face when he saw Kevin standing before him with the armoured suit. He tried to turn and flee, but a circle of pink energy surrounded his body, trapping him.

'Get the armour on him!' Kevin cried, as Gwen tried to guide P'andor back inside the suit.

'Easier said than done,' she said. Inside the sphere, P'andor glowed a brilliant shade of red. He exploded free of the trap, knocking the armour over and sending Gwen and Kevin crashing heavily into the corridor walls.

Gwen gasped as P'andor stepped closer. Behind him, Kevin touched the armour, absorbing its power once again. 'If this stuff can hold you, I'm betting it can touch you,' he muttered, lifting the armour above his head.

WHUMP!

The armour smashed into P'andor, driving him through a stone wall. Big Chill swooped down and pulled Gwen to safety, just as rubble rained down from above.

'I need to refuel,' P'andor hissed, pulling himself out from beneath the armour. His eyes fell on the nuclear rods that powered the station. They were kept in a deep pool of cold water to prevent them becoming dangerously hot. 'I must feed off the source!'

Diving into the water, P'andor began twisting the rods free. Pink power lit up Gwen's hands, but Kevin caught her by the arm. 'Forget it. Radiation level's in the red,' he warned. 'Get out, now!'

'I can do this!'

'I know you can, but you're not protected like me and Ben.'

'But –'

'Think with your head, not with your fists,' Kevin said, softly. 'That's my job.'

Gwen hesitated, then nodded her head. 'OK.'

Pulling the rods free, P'andor began to gulp them down. With each one he swallowed, his fiery frame grew larger. 'Not a meal,' he cheered, 'a feast!'

It was now or never. Big Chill and Kevin mounted a double-team attack. Kevin attacked P'andor's legs, pounding them with his metal fists. Big Chill swooped in from above, hitting him with icy blast after icy blast. P'andor barely seemed to notice the attacks.

'Guys, you can't fight him,' shouted Gwen. She was watching the fight from inside a nearby control room. 'He just fed on the uranium core. He's now a living nuclear reactor.'

'So what should we do?' Big Chill hissed.

Gwen pointed to the top of the reactor. 'Kevin, see those carbon rods? They absorb excess radiation.'

'On it!'

Kevin grabbed a rod and his body immediately changed to match it. Throwing himself at P'andor, he landed on the alien's back. P'andor began to twist and writhe, as Kevin drained his radiation powers away.

'Stop!' he yelped. 'Get ... off ... me ... now!'

P'andor was growing smaller, but he was still fighting with all his strength. 'I can't hold him on my own!' Kevin cried.

Big Chill flew down and dropped the armour beside them. 'I know someone who can!'

A green flash lit up the room, and Big Chill became ...

'Cannonbolt!'

Wrapping his body around Kevin, P'andor and the armour, Cannonbolt curled into a tight ball. He bounced around the station for a few moments, before rolling to a stop.

Uncurling, he saw that P'andor was back inside the metal suit.

'How'd you know I'd be able to absorb the armour and morph it around P'andor?' Kevin asked.

Cannonbolt blinked, confused. 'Is that what you did?'

With a groan, P'andor began to move. Kevin smiled. 'Don't worry about him.' He rolled the armoured figure over, revealing his hands were joined together behind his back. 'I made some alterations to the suit!'

A short while later, two Plumbers marched P'andor onto their ship. 'We'll make sure he's deported back to his home planet,' one of them said, as the ship's doors began to close.

'That leaves two of Aggregor's

former captives at large,' Ben said. 'Hopefully, they'll be a little more cooperative than P'andor,' Gwen nodded.

With a roar of engines, the ship blasted off. The three heroes watched it until it was just a distant dot against the dark night sky.

'Mayday! Mayday! Mayday!' bellowed one of the Plumbers on the spaceship. 'We're under attack!'

The communications console exploded before the message could be sent. Trapped inside an energy prison, P'andor could only watch as a hole was torn in the side of the spaceship.

Screaming, the Plumbers flipped over and over as they were sucked through the hole and into outer space. P'andor knew who was behind the attack. There was nobody else it could be.

Aggregor appeared on the other side of the energy field.

'Did you really think you could escape from me?' he demanded.

Without waiting for an answer, he switched off P'andor's energy prison. Taking hold of his armour, Aggregor dragged the helpless P'andor across the floor, and up a boarding ramp. The monster's laughter echoed along the corridors as he dumped the prisoner in the dungeon of his own ship.

Three of his escaped captives had now been recaptured. Only two remained. A nasty smile spread across Aggregor's face. This was going to be fun!